Little Sparkles

Party in the garden

Collect all the

LITTLE SPARKLES

Little Sparkles

Party in the Garden

Emily Moon

Illustrated by Aaron Zenz

SCHOLASTIC

First published in the UK in 2012 by Scholastic Children's Books
An imprint of Scholastic Ltd
Euston House, 24 Eversholt Street
London, NW1 1DB, UK
Registered office: Westfield Road, Southam, Warwickshire, CV47 0RA
SCHOLASTIC and associated logos are trademarks and/or
registered trademarks of Scholastic Inc.
Series created by Working Partners Ltd.

Text copyright © Working Partners Ltd., 2012
Illustration copyright © Aaron Zenz, 2012

ISBN 978 1407 12456 8

Printed and bound by CPI Group (UK) Ltd., Croydon, CR0 4YY
Papers used by Scholastic Children's Books
are made from wood grown in sustainable forests.

1 3 5 7 9 10 8 6 4 2

www.scholastic.co.uk/zone

With special thanks to Dawn McNiff

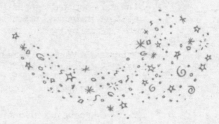

To Poppy and Lola, with all my love

Dear Holly & Rose,

Hooray! Hooray!
It's my birthday!
Come to my house
on Sunday at 2 o'clock
for a party.
There'll be delicious food
and exciting games,
and to top it all off
we'll be making hats.
          Love,
          Jenny

1

What a Mess!

"If we leave Jenny's present on the doorstep," said Rose, pushing open the gate and walking up the flower-lined path, "then she'll have a lovely surprise when she opens the door."

"Oh, yes!" said her twin sister Holly. She clapped her hands together, making her bangles jingle. "She might even think it's a magical present."

The twins put the pink, glittery parcel

down on the step. They rang the doorbell and crouched behind a cherry tree by the door.

"Look at all these fallen blossoms," whispered Holly. "We could shower Jenny with them when she comes out."

"Good idea," said Rose, gathering up handfuls of the soft flowers.

Jenny opened the door. She was wearing a white party dress embroidered with tiny strawberries. A matching bow was fastened to her brown ponytail. Jenny bent down to pick up the present.

"Who could this be from?" she wondered.

Rose and Holly jumped out from behind the cherry tree. "Happy birthday!" they called out and scattered the blossoms high in the air. They fluttered down like butterflies and landed in Jenny's ponytail.

Jenny giggled. "You two are the

best!" she said.

"You look so pretty, Jenny," said Holly. "Like a proper princess!"

"Thank you," said Jenny, giving a little curtsey. "I really like your party dresses too."

The twins twirled around. Their long toffee-coloured plaits swung out, and their blue silk skirts shimmered in the sunlight. They looked exactly the same, except that Rose wore a pink watch and Holly wore a green one. Rose glanced at hers.

"Half past one," she read. "We know the party doesn't start until two o'clock, but Mum had some shopping to do so she dropped us off early."

"I'm glad you're here," said Jenny. "Everything's nearly ready, but you could help me take the last things out to the garden."

She led Rose and Holly into the kitchen, where they found a tray piled

with candy-striped paper cups and a jug
of pink juice.

"It's Raspberry Fizz," said Jenny. "And
for tea, we're having chocolate-button
sandwiches, fairy cakes and fudge ice
cream."

"Yummy," said Rose.

"...in my tummy!" said Holly.

Jenny laughed. "I can't wait." She

twirled around. "And we're making hats! We've got lots of things for decorating them – sequins, paper flowers, ribbons and stars. There are even jelly sweets to stick on as jewels."

"Ooh, I'm going to make a fairy-queen crown," said Rose.

"I'm doing a pirate hat," said Holly.

The twins carried the tray and jug to the back door, and Jenny brought a big bowl of marshmallows. Through the window, Holly and Rose caught a glimpse of the garden.

The climbing frame had a banner saying "HAPPY BIRTHDAY!" draped across it.

Big, sugar-pink balloons were tied to the swing set, and a ball pit full of colourful balls sat in the shade of some apple trees.

"Wowee!" said Holly. "It looks perfect."

They pushed open the back door and stepped out into the sunshine.

But Jenny's face fell. "What's happened?" she cried.

Rose and Holly gasped. In front of the rose arch were long tables, each covered in a pink tablecloth. But the tablecloths were all higgledy-piggledy, and they could see lots of things scattered on the ground.

The girls put down what they were carrying and ran over.

On the tea table, the chocolate-button sandwiches were squashed, the icing had been scraped off the fairy cakes, and there were crisps all over the lawn.

"Oh no," cried Holly. "What a mess!"

They hurried over to the party-bag table – and it was even worse. The silver party bags were torn open. Everything had tumbled out of them, and the grass was littered with sugar mice, sweetie-necklaces and glitter pens.

"Urgh – look at the hat-making table!" shrieked Rose. "Are those SLUGS?"

They all rushed over to look.

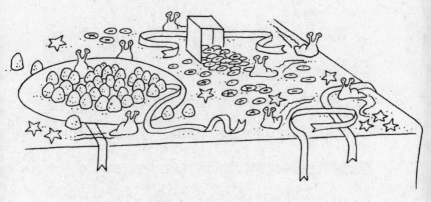

The slugs were wriggling over the ribbons and sequins, leaving criss-cross trails of slime.

"The other guests will be here soon," said Jenny. She looked like she was going to cry. "My perfect party is ruined!"

2

Sparkle Magic

"What on earth has happened?" wondered Jenny's mum, when the girls showed her the mess. She frowned thoughtfully. "The last few days have been very windy. Maybe everything's been blown about."

Jenny sniffed. "All my friends were so excited about coming to my party, but no one will have any fun now."

"Poor Jenny," said Rose, hugging her

friend. "Don't worry – we'll help tidy up." She picked up the crumpled pass-the-parcel and began retying the ribbon.

"Yes," agreed Holly. "Why don't you and your mum take the cakes and party bags indoors and fix them. Rose and I will tidy up the garden."

"That's very sweet of you, girls," said Jenny's mum. "If we work together we can sort out this muddle before everyone arrives." She hurried off towards the house, carrying the cake stand.

Jenny wiped her eyes and gave the twins a watery smile. "Thank you for helping," she said, and followed her mum indoors with a tray of ruined party bags.

"OK," said Rose, "let's get going."

Just then, the cloth on the craft table flapped in the breeze, sending more ribbons and feathers tumbling on to the grass.

"Oh dear," said Holly. "We'd better start by taping the cloths down – before they get blown away too."

Holly reached out for the sticky tape on the tabletop. But the tape roll whisked away from her and hovered in mid-air all by itself. A strip of tape peeled off, flew to a corner of the table and fixed down the tablecloth.

The twins gasped and rubbed their eyes.

"Did that tape really...?" began Holly. But then they stopped still. What was that odd tinkling noise? It sounded like tiny, faraway bells.

"What a pretty sound," said Holly.

"It's coming from under the table!" said Rose. "Shall we take a look? One, two, three..."

They stuck their heads under the tablecloth, and were dazzled by flashes of light.

"Wow!" gasped Holly, blinking.

Five tiny, brightly coloured creatures were floating in the air – a light-blue puppy, a little white pony with purple spots on her back, a teeny-weeny yellow kitten, a turtle with a rainbow shell, and a tiny pink bunny. They were all fluffy and glittery, and so small they could have sat in the twins' hands. Each one carried a little party bag.

The miniature animals didn't seem to notice the twins. They were too busy chattering away in sweet little voices, making the tinkling sound the twins had heard.

"Such a brilliant idea to make party hats," said the pony, prancing in the air.

"Lovely, pretty hats!" said the kitten in a sing-song voice.

"And did you see the sweets? I just love sweetie-necklaces," said the turtle. He sighed. "And now it's all spoiled."

"Um ... hello?" said Rose.

The animals jumped. The turtle flew inside his shell. The bunny hid behind her ears.

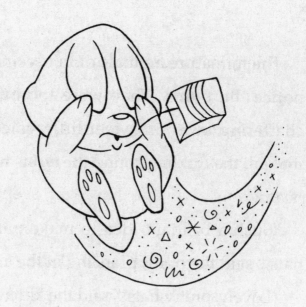

"Oh no, they can see us!" came the turtle's muffled voice.

"It's OK – don't be scared," said Rose.

"We won't hurt you," said Holly.

The twins crawled under the table. The little puppy floated nearer to them, leaving a trail of blue glitter behind him.

"It's true," he yapped. "You can see us!"

The twins looked at each other, and then back at the puppy. "Of course we can!"

"Well, um, it's nice to meet you," said the puppy politely. "But how very surprising! No one has ever seen us before."

"But who *are* you?" asked Rose.

"We," said the puppy, wagging his tiny tail, "are the Little Sparkles!"

3

Pesky Poopers

The other Little Sparkles came closer, and stared at the twins with big eyes.

The kitten bobbed over to Holly in a shimmer of yellow glitter. She rubbed her soft head on Holly's hand, purring.

"That's Tikki the kitten," said the puppy. "My name is Peppy. This is Bubbles the bunny." The little rabbit giggled shyly. "And please meet Tubbs the turtle and Princess the pony."

"Hello," chorused the twins, smiling.

"I'm Rose, and this is my sister, Holly," said Rose.

"Am I seeing double," asked Tubbs, rubbing his eyes, "or do you two look exactly the same?"

"We do," laughed Holly, "except Rose has a pink watch, and I have a green one. It's the only way you can tell us apart."

"Wow! Identical twins," purred Tikki. "How special!"

"Yes, and even more special because you can see us," said Peppy, giving Rose his paw to shake. "Little Sparkles are usually invisible to people."

"But what do Little Sparkles *do*?" asked Holly, stroking Tikki with her little finger.

"It's simple," said Peppy. "We make sure parties are really fun."

"So can you help us fix poor Jenny's party?" asked Rose. "Everything's in such a mess."

The Little Sparkles suddenly looked serious. Bubbles hid behind her ears again with a squeak.

"That's why we're here," explained

Peppy. His tail drooped sadly. "You see, there's a group of naughty Party Poopers hiding in Jenny's garden somewhere. They're the ones who've messed up her party!"

"Party Poopers?!" said Rose and Holly, at the same time. "What are *they*?"

"Party Poopers are pests," said Peppy with a shudder. "They use mean magic to poop parties."

Rose gasped. "They ruin parties *on purpose*?"

"Oh yes," miaowed Tikki sadly. "We used to be able to stop them, but they've got so good at messing up parties that we can't beat them any more."

"They're very full of themselves now," said Tubbs. "They think they're super-duper Poopers."

"But that's horrid. We can't let them poop Jenny's party," said Holly.

"No way," said Rose. "We're going to help you stop them."

Peppy chased his tail. "I knew it! You girls really are special. That must be why you can see us – so you can help us beat the Poopers."

"Come on!" cried Holly. "Let's get started."

In a shower of multicoloured glitter, the five Little Sparkles zipped out from under the table, followed by the twins.

They whirled and looped in the air so fast that Rose and Holly felt quite dizzy watching them. Then they floated over the hat-making table, which was still crawling with slugs.

"Everyone ready?" Peppy called out to the other Little Sparkles.

"What do you think they're going to

do?" whispered Rose. The twins linked arms and held their breath.

"GO!" barked Peppy.

The Little Sparkles pulled matching party blowers out of their party bags and blew together like a tiny brass band.

Instantly, all the slugs got in a clumsy queue and slithered to the edge of the table. One by one they plopped down on to the grass and roly-polyed away into the flower beds. Holly and Rose clapped.

"Brilliant!" said Holly. "Soon everything will be perfect for the party again." She began tidying the ribbons and feathers.

"Oh no, it won't," snapped a grumpy voice. "Stop ruining our lovely mess."

The twins turned round. Standing on the lawn was a tiny figure, no bigger than the Little Sparkles. He was knobbly and blobby and had sticky grey skin like he was made from mouldy Play-Doh. His arms and legs were short and fat, and he had a short stubby tail and a frowning, screwed-up face.

"A Party Pooper!" gasped Rose.

The Party Pooper stuck out his tongue at the girls. "Bleurgh! You can't stop us!"

4

A Poopy Problem

"Look," cried Holly. "More Party Poopers!"

She pointed to four grey blobs squirming out from under a bush. They were covered with feathers and sequins. One had pink icing all over his face.

"Ha, ha!" one of them squawked. "I hate parties. Let's make sure this one's rubbish."

They bounced off in five different directions.

"Oh no," squeaked Tikki. "They're going to poop everything!"

"Not while we're here," said Holly. "Let's catch them!"

The twins raced after a trail of feathers left by one of the Party Poopers, with the Little Sparkles flying after them. They found him on the climbing frame, trying to rip down the "HAPPY BIRTHDAY!" banner. He was shouting out a song:

"Numpty bumpty,
yippedy yee,
I'll ruin this party –
just you see!"

"Stop it!" ordered Rose. "Leave that banner alone."

"Stop it! Stop it!" mimicked the Party Pooper. "No, I won't – and you can't make me." He hopped from foot to foot, waggling his stubby tail.

"That banner is tied properly," said Rose. "You won't pull it down with your silly dancing about."

"Dancing? I'm not dancing!" yelled the Party Pooper. "Dancing is fun – and I HATE fun!" He made a face like he wanted to be sick. "I hate parties and cake and sunshine and sugar mice and anything nice – but I especially hate dancing!"

"Oh really?" said Holly. She turned and whispered to Rose and the Little Sparkles. "If we keep him busy talking to us, he won't be able to run off and do more pooping."

She called up to the Party Pooper. "Well, you looked like you were dancing to me. You were doing the same dance I do when I'm happy. Like this..." She did some ballet steps, leaping gracefully from foot to foot and holding out her arms.

Rose joined in too. Tikki whistled a happy tune, and all the other Little

Sparkles did a floating dance around the climbing frame. Bubbles bounced up and down, Princess pranced prettily, and Tubbs kicked his feet in and out of his shell.

"Argh! No!" squawked the Party Pooper. "I was NOT dancing! I am NOT happy!" He jumped off the climbing frame, landing in a belly flop on the lawn, and stomped sulkily towards the house. "I'm not staying here with you silly smilers!" he yelled over his shoulder. And, with one bounce, the Party Pooper disappeared down a drain.

"Hooray!" cheered Rose. "Now he can't ruin Jenny's party any more."

"And it's all thanks to you two," said Peppy. He held up a little furry paw, and the twins gave him a high five.

"Yeah, you'd better watch out, you poopy Poopers," called Tubbs. "We've got twin power on our side now."

"We promise to do our best," laughed Holly. Then she glanced at her green watch. "Jenny's party starts in a few minutes – and there are still four Poopers to find!"

5

Balloon Hullabaloo

"Over there!" said Rose, pointing.

Two Poopers were sitting on top of the swing frame. They scowled and shook their fists at the pink balloons, which were tied to the frame with violet ribbons.

"Look," cried Holly. "The Poopers have stolen the scissors from the hat-making table. I think they're going to—"

SNIP!

One of the Party Poopers cut right through a ribbon. The balloon attached to it floated up into a tree, snagging on one of the branches.

"All these party things are making me itch," grumbled the other Pooper, rubbing his flubby grey tummy. "Get rid of another balloon!"

"You stop that!" shouted Rose. "Those balloons belong to Jenny."

"Can't tell us what to do," said the Pooper, snipping another ribbon. "Bye bye, silly balloons – DON'T come back soon."

"Charge!" yelled Peppy.

The Little Sparkles flew at the Poopers.

But the Poopers were too quick. They each grabbed a balloon and used them to bat the Little Sparkles away.

"I'm going to cut all the ribbons," yelled the Pooper holding the scissors. "Snip, snip, snip!"

"But it's my turn," the other Pooper pouted. "Give the scissors to me!"

"No – I'm not sharing!" the first

Pooper shrieked. He held the scissors high in the air.

"Be careful," called Rose. "Scissors are dangerous."

But the Poopers took no notice. The Pooper who wanted a turn at cutting the ribbons lunged for the scissors. The other Pooper shrieked and swung them out of his reach.

BANG!

The sharp points of the scissors had jabbed into a balloon. The Poopers jumped in fright and nearly fell off the swing frame. They clung to each other, whimpering, as the scissors fell safely on to the lawn.

"Rubbishy balloons," one of the Poopers grumbled. "And rubbishy birthdays! We'll poop them all."

"But birthdays are brilliant," said Rose. "Everyone knows that."

"Birthdays – pah!" said the other Pooper. "Throw them in the bin. There's nothing good about them."

"Oh yes, there is," said Holly. "Like birthday cake."

"And playing games," added Rose.

"And the song!" squeaked Tikki. "That's my favourite bit of all." She

began to sing "Happy Birthday". The
twins and the other Little Sparkles joined
in. Tikki conducted them with her tail.

"No, no," shrieked the Poopers. "Stop
that nasty niceness!" They shoved their
grey fingers into their ears.

"See how much they hated that,"

whispered Rose. "So let's..."

"...sing and sing!" finished Holly. "Maybe it'll make them go away."

The twins held hands and led the Little Sparkles in another loud chorus.

"Horrible happiness!" one of the Poopers yelled. "We've had enough!"

They both jumped off the swing frame, landing in a splat, one on top of the other.

Then they tumbled together,

howling and fighting, across the garden. They squashed themselves as flat as they could, wriggled under the fence, and were gone.

"Well done, girls," said Peppy. "That's three Poopers down. Only two to go."

"And I know where they are!" said Rose.

She pointed over at the ball pit. The colourful balls that filled it were flying through the air, into the neighbour's garden.

SPLASH! SPLASH!

"What's making that noise?" Holly wondered.

They all rushed and peered over the

fence. The balls were floating on a big green pond.

"Yuck," Rose said, "look how slimy it is."

"Right, that's it," said Holly crossly. "We've got to stop them!"

6

The Naughtiest Pooper

There was chanting coming from the ball pit:

"Into the slime, plop plop plop!
Balls all gone, this party's a flop!"

The twins and the Little Sparkles rushed over. Inside were the final two Poopers. They had thrown so many balls into the pond that the ball pit was half empty.

"Too late," shouted one of the Poopers, hurling another ball over the fence. "We're throwing all the fun away."

"Yeah," agreed the other Pooper. "We're sinking this poxy party to the bottom of the pond."

"Oh no, you're not. We'll stop you," said Rose and Holly.

They stood in front of the fence like goalkeepers, ready to catch the balls before they went over. Rose jumped high and grabbed a red ball, but the Poopers changed tactics and pelted the balls at the Little Sparkles instead.

"Be careful, Little Sparkles!" called Holly.

The Little Sparkles zoomed about quickly, dodging the balls. Tubbs hid in his shell and Tikki leapt into a tree.

"They are so mean," neighed Princess, kicking a ball away with one of her hoofs. "Help us, Holly and Rose! How can we stop them?"

The twins frowned. "Well, the first Pooper hated dancing," said Holly slowly.

"And the next two Poopers hated singing," added Rose.

Holly's eyes widened. "That's it!" she cried. "They hate having fun. So if we have fun, it'll make the Poopers go away."

Rose grinned and the Little Sparkles cheered.

"Good thinking," yapped Peppy.

"Time for some fun, everyone!" said Holly.

The twins grabbed a handful of party blowers from a table. They skipped around, blowing as hard as they could.

PARP! TOOT! PARP!

The Little Sparkles laughed at the silly squeaky sounds, but the Poopers cringed.

"Argh – horrible fun!" one of them groaned. They covered their squashy ears.

"Now we can't hear you," the other Pooper boasted. "So there!"

"Come on," said Rose. "Let's make the music louder."

The Little Sparkles reached inside their

party bags. In a shower of sparkles, they each pulled out a party blower and flew around the Poopers, blowing hard.

PARP! BEEP! TOOT!

The Poopers squirmed and moaned until, with an ear-splitting screech, one leapt out of the ball pit.

"Yuck," he shouted. "I'm getting out of here!" He bounded over the fence and vanished.

The final Pooper scowled at the twins.

"Well, I'm staying," he snapped. "You wait and see what I can do all by myself."

He did a cartwheel across the lawn, and leapt up on to the craft table.

"Meddly-muddly! Meddly-muddly!" he said, stamping around on the tissue-paper flowers and ribbons with his big, blobby feet. "Marvellous, messy, mucky muddle."

The twins ran over with the Little Sparkles.

"Quick, Holly – I've got an idea," said Rose.

She ran over to the hat-making table and grabbed the sticky tape. Unravelling a long strip, she held on to the end and then threw the roll to Holly, who caught it neatly.

"Now let's tie him up," cried Rose.

They ran around the table, winding the tape round and round the Pooper.

"Yes – get him, girls!" barked Peppy.

But the Pooper struggled hard. He wriggled and kicked and fought. Then, with a loud yell, he snapped the tape and broke free, chanting:

"I'm all undone
So you haven't won,
And I can still spoil the fun!"

He kicked a box of sequins off the table, and threw handfuls of feathers in the air.

Holly and Rose shared a worried look.

"This Pooper's much worse than the others," said Holly. "How are we ever going to get rid of him?"

7

A Super-Duper Pooper

The Pooper skidded along the table on the spilled decorations, showering the lawn with sparkles. He was covered from head to foot with sequins and feathers.

"Everything's getting stuck to him," said Rose. "He must be sticky from the tape."

"He looks funny," laughed Holly.

"I do NOT look funny, you ninnies!" yelled the Pooper. He shook himself hard, and a pink feather dangled over his face. He wriggled his nose to get it off, but the feather tickled him and he chuckled. "Hee hee!"

"Oh, listen," said Rose. "You made a happy noise."

"Yes," said Holly. "You just laughed."

"I did not!" snapped the Pooper, from behind the feather. "Party poopers *never* laugh. No, I was just saying 'yuck'. Yuck, yuck, yuck, YUCK!"

But the feather tickled him again, and he giggled.

"Ha ha hee!" The Pooper put his hands over his mouth in surprise.

"You see," said Rose, "you're having fun. You can't help it."

A puff of pink mist surrounded the Pooper. It wafted and sparkled, and his grey body glowed with rainbow colours. He looked down at himself, his eyes wide.

"What's happening to him?" Holly wondered in a whisper.

A big sunshiny smile spread across the Pooper's face, and he started laughing.

"Ha ha ha!" The more he laughed, the more he sparkled. "Ha ha! Hee hee!"

It was the jolliest sound the twins had ever heard, and they couldn't help but join in. The Little Sparkles swirled around them, dancing and cheering.

POOF!

There was a shower-burst of glittering hundreds and thousands, and the Pooper changed into a little orange chick. On his head was a fluffy tuft of feathers that looked just like a party hat.

"He's turned into a Little Sparkle!"
gasped Rose.

"Hip, hip. . ." the Little Sparkles called
together.

". . .hooray!" finished the twins. They
held hands and danced in a circle around
the little chick as he fluttered in the air.
The Little Sparkles whirled and twirled
above their heads, giggling delightedly.

"Wow," said Holly, flopping down on to the grass. "That was proper magic."

Peppy reached into his party bag and pulled out an orange balloon tied with a long ribbon. He passed it to the new Little Sparkle, while the other Little Sparkles chanted together:

"Spread the lovely party joy to every little girl and boy.
No more a grumpy Party Pooper, make all parties super duper."

As they chanted, the balloon magically blew itself up and rose into the air.

"Whee!" cried the new Little Sparkle.

He held on tightly to the
ribbon as the balloon floated
gently upwards.

"Where's he going?"
asked Rose.

"Now he's a
Little Sparkle,
he's off to help
make someone
else's party happy
and fun," said Peppy.

"Goodbye," Holly called after the
chick. "Good luck!"

They all waved as the Little Sparkle
drifted slowly away.

Tubbs floated in front of Holly and

Rose. "We couldn't have got rid of the Poopers without you two," he said. He tipped his shell forward in a little bow. "You saved the party."

"But we haven't saved the party yet, have we?" said Holly. She pointed at her green watch. "Jenny's other friends will be here any minute, and look – everything's still in a right muddle."

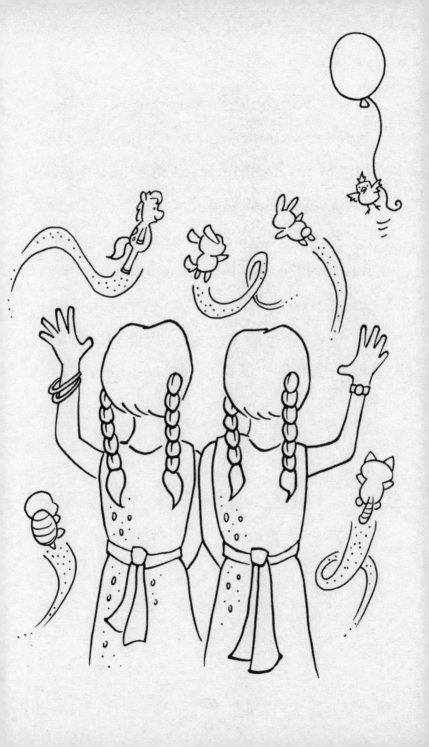

8

A Perfect Party

"It's OK," chorused the Little Sparkles.

"We can fix this mess in no time," added Peppy.

The Little Sparkles looped-the-loop in the air, sprinkling the garden with glittery hundreds and thousands. The twins watched with wide eyes as the balloons flew down from the trees and arranged themselves in bunches again.

The ribbons, glitter and paper flowers

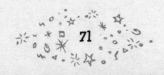

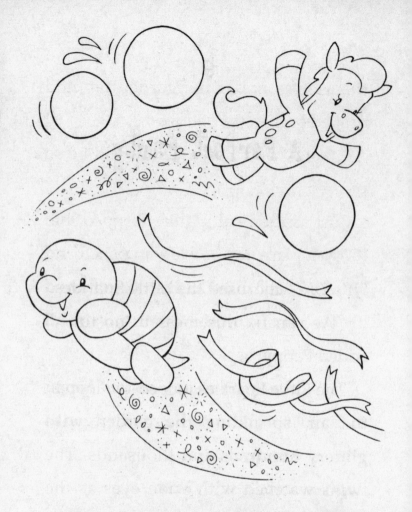

whirled up in the air and settled in their
right places on the hat-making table. The
balls flew out of the pond, washed

themselves under the garden tap and nestled back in the ball pit.

"Wow," said Rose. "Jenny will be so pleased!"

Just as the final sequin dropped into its right place, the back door opened and Jenny stepped outside. She was followed by her mum and the other guests, all dressed in party clothes.

"It's time for us to go," barked Peppy to the twins. The Little Sparkles began to float up and away.

"Goodbye," cried Holly.

"Will we see you again?" asked Rose.

"Of course," Peppy called down to them. "Whenever there's a party, the

Little Sparkles are sure to be there!"

And in a sparkling flash, the Little Sparkles vanished, leaving behind just a faint rainbow shimmer in the air.

Jenny skipped across the lawn. "Oh, Holly and Rose," she said, pulling them both into a hug. "Everything looks lovely again. Thank you!"

"Gosh, you *have* worked hard," smiled Jenny's mum, bustling over. "How did you manage to clear everything up so quickly?"

The twins glanced at each other, unsure what to say, but Jenny's mum turned away when one of the guests gave a cry.

"Look!" exclaimed a girl in a red dress. "One of your balloons has escaped, Jenny." She pointed up at the orange balloon, floating away with the new Little Sparkle underneath. All the guests blinked up at the sky.

Rose and Holly smiled at each other.

"Lucky they can't see the little chick!" whispered Holly.

The party was soon in full swing. The guests got busy making hats and playing games in the soft summer sunshine.

The garden rang with the sound of laughter and happy chatter.

Holly and Rose each linked an arm
through Jenny's.

"Race you to the ball pit," said Holly.

The three girls sprinted across the grass and dived into the heap of multicoloured balls.

"Yippee!" said Jenny. "This party's magical!"

Rose grinned. "It's got Sparkle magic!"

Don't miss the other

books in the series!

Little Sparkles

Party at the Pool

Have fun with these tiny magical animals!

Em...

Little Sparkles

Party on the Pirate Ship

Have fun with these tiny magical animals!

Emily Moon

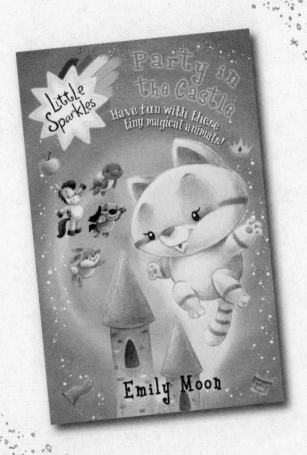